The MYSTERIOUS BENEDICT SOCIETY

Mr. Benedict's Book of Perplexing Puzzles, Elusive Enigmas, and Curious Conundrums

TRENTON LEE STEWART

Illustrations by Diana Sudyka

Megan Tingley Books

LITTLE, BROWN AND COMPANY

New York   Boston

I WISH TO THANK THE WRITER AND RIDDLER JOSH GREENHUT, THE EXCELLENT EDITORS JULIE SCHEINA AND MEGAN TINGLEY, THE CONSCIENTIOUS COPY EDITOR BARBARA BAKOWSKI, AND THE CLEVER ANCIENT PERSONS WHO INVENTED PAPER AND INK. THIS BOOK WOULD NOT EXIST WITHOUT THEM.

Little, Brown and Company

Hachette Book Group
1290 Avenue of the Americas, New York, NY 10104
Visit us at lb-kids.com.

Little, Brown and Company is a division of Hachette Book Group, Inc.
The Little, Brown name and logo are trademarks of Hachette Book Group, Inc.

The publisher is not responsible for websites (or their content) that are not owned by the publisher.

First Paperback Edition: June 2016
First published in hardcover in October 2011 by Little, Brown and Company

The Library of Congress has cataloged the hardcover edition as follows:
Stewart, Trenton Lee.
The mysterious Benedict society : Mr. Benedict's book of perplexing puzzles, elusive enigmas, and curious conundrums / by Trenton Lee Stewart ; illustrated by Diana Sudyka.
p. cm.—(The Mysterious Benedict Society)
ISBN 978-0-316-18193-8
1. Puzzles—Juvenile literature. 2. Riddles, Juvenile. 3. Amusements—Juvenile literature. I. Title.
GV1493.S813 2011
793.73—dc22   2011010259

Paperback ISBN 978-0-316-39475-8

10 9 8 7 6 5 4 3 2 1

APS

Printed in China

Book design by Georgia Rucker Design

Dear Reader,

I am aware that certain individuals have become acquainted with the adventures — and even the personal stories — of the remarkable children who call themselves the Mysterious Benedict Society. Furthermore, it is my understanding that these individuals have developed a wish to see their own wits tested, much as the wits of the Society members were tested before the Society was formed. If you are reading these words, it is likely you are just such an individual. Therefore, I urge you to put on your thinking cap (or if you are already wearing your thinking cap, to adjust it so that it rests most comfortably upon your head), for with the aid — indeed, the considerable contributions — of the Society members themselves, as well as a few of my associates, I have compiled the manual you now hold in your hands: a compressed and highly portable collection of mental challenges. May you find them rewarding!

Best regards,

Mr. Benedict

P.S. If, perchance, this volume is not part of your personal collection, please complete the exercises in a separate notebook so that others who wish to attempt these challenges may do so.

She continued handing out the test. Child after child received it with trembling fingers, and child after child, upon looking at the questions, turned pale, or red, or a subtle shade of green. By the time the pencil woman dropped the pages upon his desk, dread was making Reynie's stomach flop like a fish. And for good reason — the questions were impossible.

Table of Contents

PUZZLES, ENIGMAS, AND CONUNDRUMS

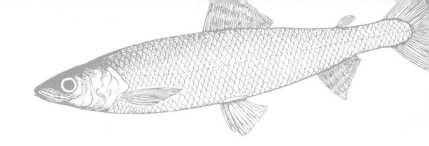

ARCHIVAL MATERIALS

HELPFUL RESOURCES

"The Mysterious Benedict Society,"

Constance said, rising as she spoke.

Then she left the room,
apparently convinced that
no more discussion was necessary.

And, as it turned out, she was right.

What brought together the members of the Mysterious Benedict Society? One might say it was our advertisement. I would argue, however, that there was also something else, something unspoken hiding in plain sight, which most had failed to detect. Can you see what it was?

CLASSIFIED ADVERTISEMENTS

HELP ANTED
Administrative Assistant
Only those who dare not defy need apply.

THE INSTITUTE OF ACCOUNTING

EMERGENCY HYGIENE SEMINAR
Are you touching this newspaper right now? Because it's covered in germs!

Sickness lurks like a hungry predator in every nook and cranny. Learn ow to protect yourself.

Mondays at 8 PM

THE ASCOT TOWER

SICK OF BAD APPLES?
We are not and never have been government-run! Bring the kiddies and get our worm-free guarantee.

JIMMY'S
APPLE P CKING & CORN MAZE
THE ORCHARD IN THE COUNTRY

Call 555-1299 to place **Your Advertisement**

HERE

FREE MARKET-ING ADVICE
I can't control myself! Is your business being hit hard by the Emergency?

Well, today's your lucky day! Listen up and get my FREE MARKET-ing advice. Not just in any case, but only in certain cases!

That's right, call now to get your FREE MARKET-ing advice. Only available in certain case .

Call

555-7655
Now!

The Message
IN THE
ADVERTISEMENTS

Sometimes it is better to say nothing.

I have no character
(Though I drop them in print)
I'm inside your head
(Let me give you a hint)
I'm quiet and soft
(Not blaring and loud)
I prompt, then I sweep
To control the crowd

What am I?

_ _ _ _ _ _ _ _ _

DOTS and DASHES

*Morse code is one of the most reliable methods of
secret communication.
It may also be one of the most commonly misunderstood.*

. ‾ .. . .. ‾ . ‾ . ‾ ‾ . ‾ . ‾ ‾ ‾ ‾ . ‾ ‾ .

Only one of the Morse codes found in the
Helpful Resources at the back of this book is
the International Morse Code, as agreed upon in 1865
at the International Telegraphy Congress in Paris, France.

Which code is the right one? Enter the page number
of the official Morse code below.

◯ — —

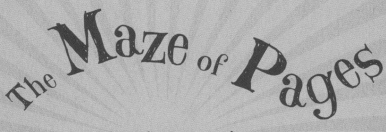

The Maze of Pages

*Dozens of variations on the maze
were created over the years.
This was one of the first.*

Navigate your way through the following pages in the
correct order. Should you find yourself stuck in the middle,
you are headed in the right direction.

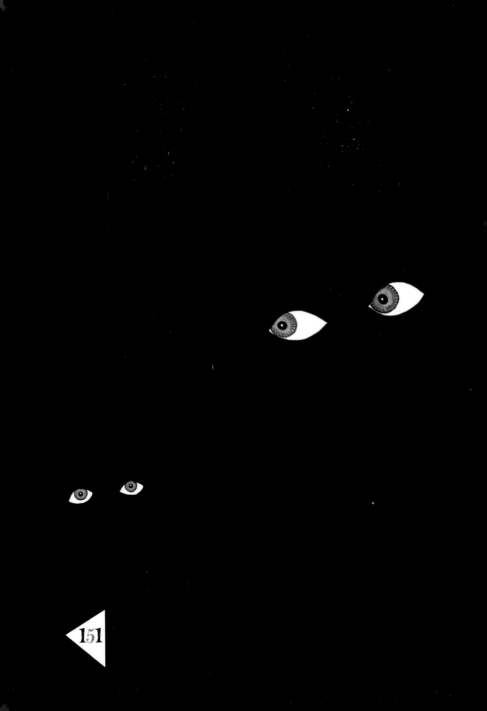

127

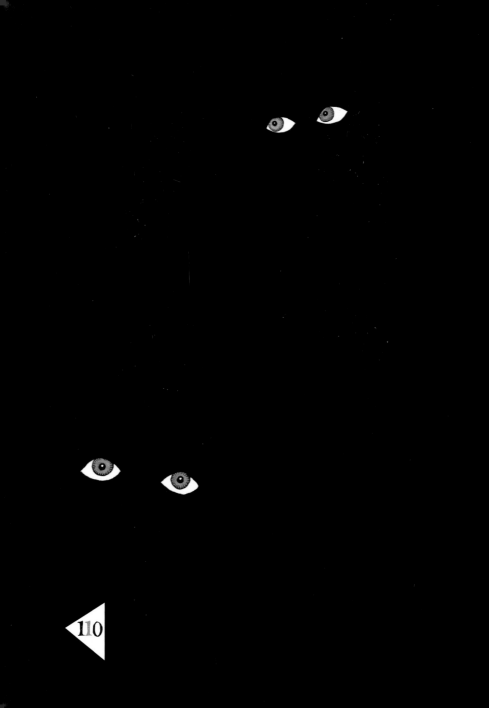

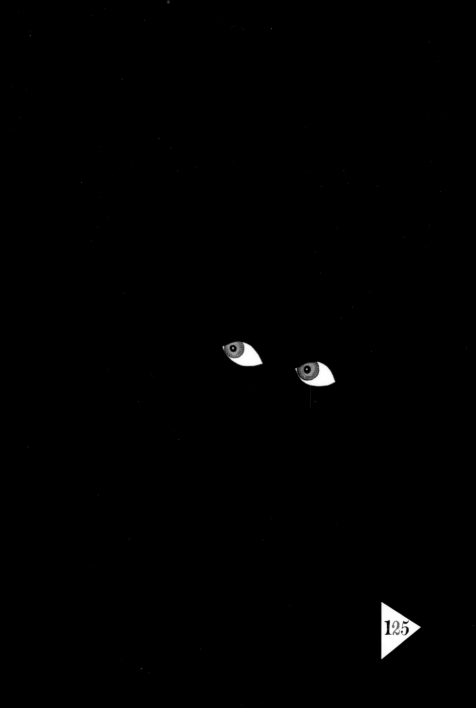

125

169

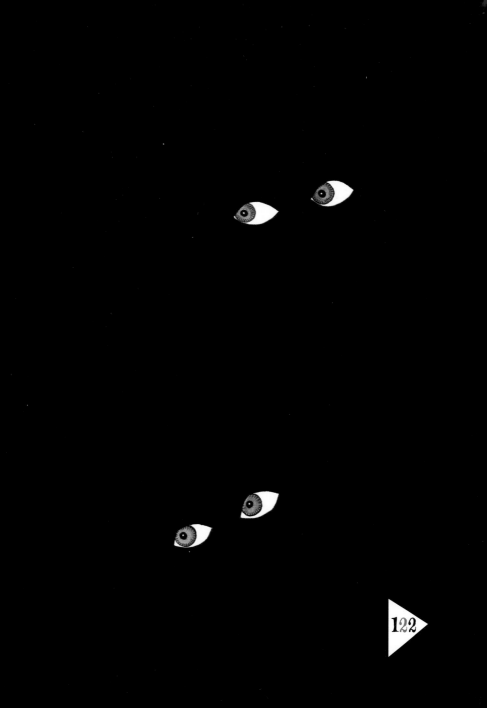

122

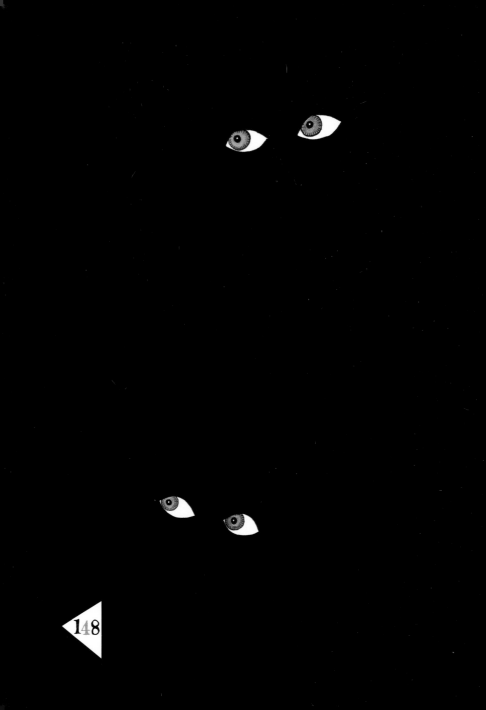

148

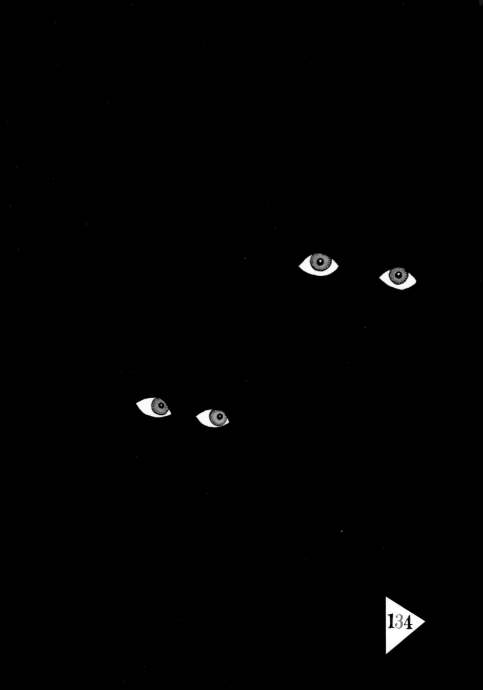

134

When Reynie was ten years old, Miss Perumal persuaded the director of Stonetown Orphanage to allow him to enter a local chess tournament. Her pride when Reynie won his age-group that day may have been matched only by my own for another, older competitor in that tournament.

Reynie Muldoon Perumal

FOUNDING MEMBER,
THE MYSTERIOUS BENEDICT SOCIETY

Achievements Learned Tamil; attained highest possible score on Mr. Benedict's tests; correctly guessed Mr. Curtain's secret password; consistently led friends with grace and wisdom against all odds

Expertise Problem solving

Habits Pacing when thinking

History Orphaned as an infant; formerly resided at Stonetown Orphanage

Family Miss Perumal, former tutor at Stonetown Orphanage, and her mother

If you have arrived here
after a long journey,
congratulations are
in order.

Record the route you followed.

__ __ __

__ __ __

__◯__

__ __ __

__ __ __

__ __ __

__ __ __

"Eavesdropping!" Number Two hissed,
crossing her arms.

"Without *me*!" Constance said,
doing the same.

Milligan came along the hallway behind
them. Playfully tapping Kate on the head
with a bundle of papers, he said,

"This is hardly appropriate behavior, young lady.
Spies have *rules*, you know."

OLD-HAG SYNDROME

Of all symptoms commonly afflicting those with
narcolepsy, a chronic condition whose sufferers fall
asleep at inappropriate times, sometimes triggered
by intense emotion and consequential cataplexy,
perhaps the most terrifying is sleep paralysis, also
known as Old-Hag Syndrome, a name thought to
have originated in the folk tradition of Newfoundland
and Labrador, the Canadian province divided by the
Strait of Belle Isle, because it causes its victims to feel
as if some dark presence is holding them down and
preventing them from moving in any way. Difficulty
breathing and heightened anxiety are characteristic.
In duration such episodes may range from several
seconds to many minutes, and may be accompanied by
vivid hallucinations of a specter or hag sitting directly
on the sufferer's chest. Reports of this terrifying
phenomenon are found in most cultures, such as in
Malta, one of the world's smallest and most densely
populated countries, where according to superstition
one must place a piece of silverware under one's pillow
to prevent haunting by an evil spirit while asleep.

DUSKWORT

Duskwort, or *Translucidus somniferum*, is a plant allegedly capable of instantly putting all who come in contact with it to sleep, although there is little evidence of its existence, beyond appearances in a handful of ancient Germanic texts and Nordic folktales, which suggest that it may once have grown in certain alpine tundra regions, such as those in northern Europe, and on the Scandinavian peninsula, which comprises Norway and Sweden. In perhaps the most famous duskwort legend, a band of invading Vikings discovers an entire village of people who have suddenly fallen asleep after merely inhaling smoke from a fire into which a tiny bit of the plant has been thrown. An especially large patch of duskwort was rumored to exist somewhere in the Russian taiga, the largest area of boreal forest in the world. So powerful was the plant thought to have been that references to its appearance, or to where it might be found, were excised from ancient texts.

SLEEPTHINKING

Rapid eye movement (REM) sleep, that period of sleep during which electrical activity in the brain is highest, is thought to aid in the solving of difficult problems, because the brain's neurons are more likely to make nonlinear, associative connections, as determined by researchers at the Sleep Institute of Belize, the northernmost Central American nation. Interestingly, those who suffer from narcolepsy access REM sleep in a matter of minutes, far more quickly than other subjects, who routinely take more than ninety minutes to reach this stage.

Too Close
TO CALL

As Constance will attest, images often prove more effective than words when attempting to put an idea in someone's head.

Each of these transmissions is intended for a different recipient. Can you determine whom?

1.

2. _ _ _ _ _ _ _ _ _ _

3. ◯ _ _ _ _ _ _ _ _ _

4. _ _ _ _ _ _ _

GEOGRAPHY TEST

You should be able to answer these questions in your sleep.

1. Which of the following is one of the world's smallest and most densely populated countries?
   a) MALTA
   b) BRAZIL
   c) LUXEMBOURG
   d) PANAMA
   e) LICHTENSTEIN

2. Where is the Strait of Belle Isle?
   a) ALASKA
   b) GIBRALTAR
   c) NEWFOUNDLAND AND LABRADOR
   d) THE PHILIPPINES
   e) SCOTLAND

3. What countries compose the
Scandinavian peninsula?
a) NORWAY, FINLAND, AND BELGIUM
b) BELGIUM AND THE NETHERLANDS
c) NORWAY AND SWEDEN
d) FINLAND AND NORWAY
e) NORWAY, SWEDEN, FINLAND, AND
ICELAND

4. What is the largest area of boreal
forest on earth?
a) AMAZON RAIN FOREST
b) AMANA RESERVE
c) REDWOOD FOREST
d) SUNDARBANS MANGROVE FOREST
e) RUSSIAN TAIGA

5. What is the northernmost country
in Central America?
a) HONDURAS
b) BELIZE
c) ARGENTINA
d) MEXICO
e) CONGO

STONETOWN TIMES

SEARCH CONTINUES FOR QUIZ CHAMP

Eleven-year-old undefeated quiz champion George Washington, also known as "Sticky" due to his remarkable ability to retain information, remains departed today after running away from home more than two weeks ago. In a note left behind for his parents, the quiz whiz said, "The psychological pressure has become inordinate." In other words, experts say, he was stressed out from winning too much. Over the last four years, Washington won nearly fifty quiz competitions, amassing thousands of dollars in cash and prizes for his family.

GEORGE "STICKY" WASHINGTON, MIDDLE, RAN AWAY
FROM HOME MORE THAN TWO WEEKS AGO.

George "Sticky" Washington

FOUNDING MEMBER,
THE MYSTERIOUS BENEDICT SOCIETY

Achievements Memorized the Stonetown Library catalog; braved the Whisperer for the sake of his friends; helped save Mr. Benedict's life

Expertise Ability to read exceptionally quickly and recall every word *exactly* (as a result, can read and write, though not necessarily speak, most major languages)

Habits Polishing spectacles when nervous; can become confused under pressure

History Former quiz-show champion; ran away from home after overhearing conversation between his mother and father

Family Mr. and Mrs. Washington, his concerned and loving parents

The Ten Man Briefcase

Rather than turn away from terrible things, it is our responsibility to learn from them. Milligan suggested this exercise after examining a briefcase he personally removed from a Ten Man.

Your task is deceptively simple. Pack the following items in the briefcase so that all of them fit.

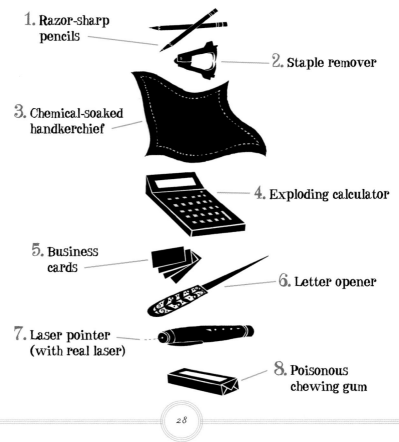

1. **Razor-sharp pencils**

2. **Staple remover**

3. **Chemical-soaked handkerchief**

4. **Exploding calculator**

5. **Business cards**

6. **Letter opener**

7. **Laser pointer (with real laser)**

8. **Poisonous chewing gum**

Pair the number of the item with its space
within the briefcase.

A ___ B ___ C ___ D ___

Ⓔ ___ F ___ G ___ H ___

That's Far Enough

It is very difficult to get close to someone like Mr. Curtain.

It is exactly 11:45 AM, and Mr. Curtain
has caught up with you at last.
In fact, his wheelchair is now only sixty feet away
from where you are securely tied up.

Much to his chagrin, however, Mr. Curtain's wheelchair
malfunctions. When he tries to move forward sixty feet, his
wheelchair goes only half that far. Of course, this means he
is now only thirty feet away. He zooms forward, but again
only half as far as he would like . . . which means he is now
merely fifteen feet from where you are a sitting duck.

In this manner, Mr. Curtain keeps lurching forward, each
time getting closer. But with every lurch, he covers only half
the distance that remains between you.

At what time will Mr. Curtain's
wheelchair crash into you?

$\underline{}\underline{O}\underline{}—\underline{}—\underline{}$

"Oh, here's a clever one.
Do you remember this question from the
first test? It reads, 'What is wrong with
this statement?' And do you know what
Constance wrote in reply? She wrote,
'What is wrong with *you*?'"

CONTRARY
Indications

Written by Number Two, inspired by you know who

After answering each of the questions on the opposite page,
complete the instructions found above. (At last!)

___ ___ ___ ___ ___ ___ ___

___ ___ ___

1. Do you prefer being called short?

       ○   ○

       Y   N

2. Do you enjoy doing laundry?

       ○   ○

       Y   N

3. Do you admire the Ten Men?

       ○   ○

       Y   N

4. Would you like a headache?

       ○   ○

       Y   N

5. Isn't it lucky that Mr. Benedict has narcolepsy?

       ○   ○

       Y   N

6. Should we shake you when you fall asleep?

       ○   ○

       Y   N

7. Do you appreciate dishonesty?

       ○   ○

       Y   N

8. Isn't waiting fun?

       ○   ○

       Y   N

9. Would you describe Mr. Curtain as pleasant?

       ○   ○

       Y   N

10. Are you the most agreeable person on earth?

       ○   ○

       Y   N

11. Don't you think you've had enough sweets?

       ○   ○

       Y   N

12. Would you say you're fond of mildew?

       ○   ○

       Y   N

13. Would you like to answer more questions?

       ○   ○

       Y   N

Rhyme Schemes and Far-Flung Plans

Every poem is a maze, whose meaning is waiting to be found.

Begin with a G, then head straight to the end

There's B and there's E, now go find the script

Which brings us to O, and from here to line two

I is for you, and after Z there's just one

Add on the L, now for what you just skipped

The last one is E, and now you are done.

The third letter is T, head to the line that is blue

The next clue is O, now by one line ascend

___ ___ ___ ___ ___ O ___ ___

MOOCHO'S
Perfect Pie

Even the simplest of challenges sometimes confound us.

Miss Perumal, her mother, Mr. Washington,
Mrs. Washington, Ms. Plugg, Rhonda Kazembe,
Number Two, Mr. Benedict, and Milligan would all very
much like a piece of Moocho Brazo's famous apple pie.

Unfortunately, because Moocho ran out of eggs,
he was able to bake only one pie today.

If you required only two pieces of pie, you could simply
make a single cut down the middle. But if everyone who
wants a piece is to enjoy one, what is the smallest number
of cuts you must make?

Observations and
COLD, HARD FACTS

*There is no place like home, especially for those
of us who know what it is like not to have one.*

Mr. Benedict's house is very old. It has three floors plus a
basement, each containing rambling hallways, a number of
rooms, and quite a few nooks and crannies. Many walls have
been knocked down and relocated over the years.
(The first floor was, until recently, a maze, but it has since
been converted into rooms.) The heating system in the
house is inefficient, with the exception of the basement,
which is climate-controlled. As a result, the third floor
often feels like a furnace while the first floor feels like the
opposite. Nearly every available surface in the house is
covered with books. In fact, according to Sticky's
calculations, there are exactly 120,136 volumes in the house.
A number of reference books can be found on the third
floor, including Greek, Latin, and Esperanto dictionaries.
Number Two's bedroom is also on the third floor. A number
of important books about narcolepsy can be found within
Mr. Benedict's study on the second floor.

Nobody has been in the room on the opposite page
in some time.

Which floor of the house is this room on?

B   1   2   3

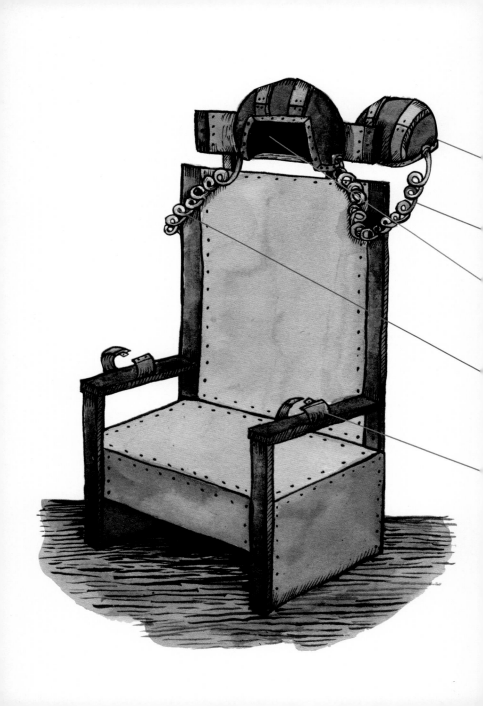

Executive brain amplifier

Reads and converts electrical impulses and conscious directions originating in the cerebral cortex and frontal lobe of Mr. Curtain's brain

Lobotomal coil

Transmits impulses from Mr. Curtain's brain to that of the Messenger

Mental collection basin

Gathers messages for transmission to the public, using tidal turbine energy

Transference helix

Transmits thoughts from the brain of the Messenger to Mr. Curtain

Restraining cuffs

Increases the sense of control enjoyed by Mr. Curtain, and monitors pulse and vital signs of the Messenger

We first became aware of Kate long before she responded to (our) advertisement in the newspaper. Indeed, we even attended the circus once and marveled at her agility.

Kate Wetherall

FOUNDING MEMBER,
THE MYSTERIOUS BENEDICT SOCIETY

Achievements Conquered the Hoop of Fire while in the circus; faced down Ten Men on numerous occasions; almost never lost patience with Constance

Expertise Physical dexterity, enhanced by fearlessness

Habits Moving around

History Mother died when she was an infant; father disappeared when she was two; ran away to join the circus at age seven

Family Milligan, her father; Moocho Brazos, caregiver, baker, former circus performer, and friend; and her falcon, Madge (also known as Her Majesty the Queen)

It was a very old house, with gray stone
walls, high arched windows, and a roof with
red shingles that glowed like embers in the
afternoon sun. Roses grew along the iron fence,
and near the house towered a gigantic elm tree,
perhaps older than the building itself, its green
leaves tinged with the first yellows of autumn.
Shaded by the elm's branches were an ivy-
covered courtyard and the stone steps upon
which they were to wait. The steps themselves
were half-covered with ivy; they seemed an
inviting place to rest.

THE
Great Kate
WEATHER MACHINE

Kate has been dreaming of doing something like this for a very long time. She even drew the pictures.

Here are your supplies!

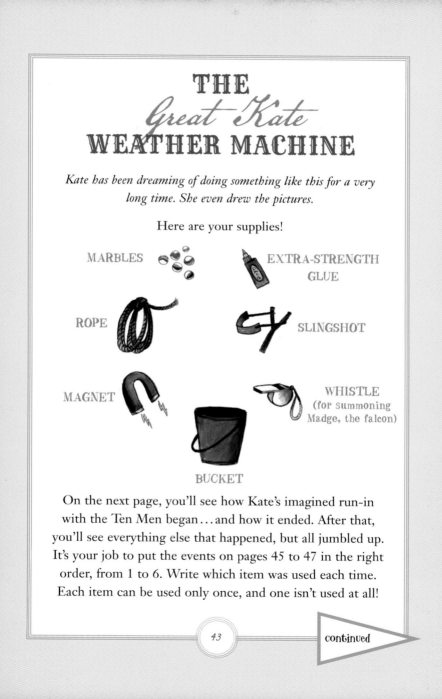

MARBLES

EXTRA-STRENGTH GLUE

ROPE

SLINGSHOT

MAGNET

WHISTLE
(for summoning Madge, the falcon)

BUCKET

On the next page, you'll see how Kate's imagined run-in with the Ten Men began...and how it ended. After that, you'll see everything else that happened, but all jumbled up. It's your job to put the events on pages 45 to 47 in the right order, from 1 to 6. Write which item was used each time. Each item can be used only once, and one isn't used at all!

continued

Place in order _____

Item used _____

Place in order _____

Item used _____

continued ▷

Kate seemed to have doubled in size. She had drawn back her broad shoulders and set her jaw, and something in her stance called to mind the contained ferocity of a lioness. But it was the fierceness in Kate's bright blue eyes that had the most striking effect. The sort of look that made you thankful she wasn't your enemy.

"It's not going to be over,"

Kate said firmly,

"until we *say* so."

Mr. Curtain's CONTROLS

We may never know the function of every button, lever, and pedal on my brother Ledroptha's wheelchair. But let us try.

Off the coast of Scotland, there is an island with an abandoned village that you will surely recall. The following instructions were found near the grain silo.

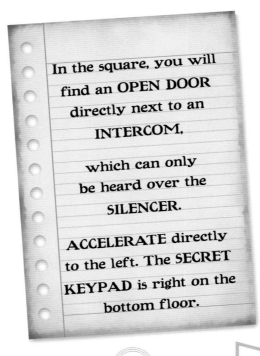

In the square, you will find an OPEN DOOR directly next to an INTERCOM,

which can only be heard over the SILENCER.

ACCELERATE directly to the left. The SECRET KEYPAD is right on the bottom floor.

continued

If this is the armrest of Mr. Curtain's wheelchair . . .

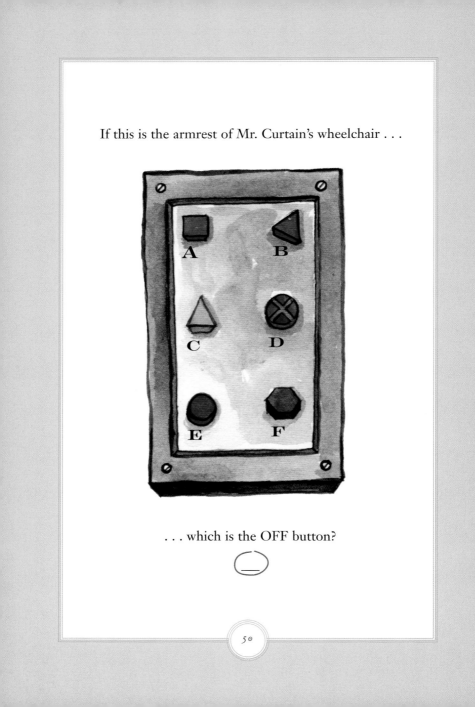

. . . which is the OFF button?

L.I.V.E.

The Learning Institute for the Very Enlightened

"Broadening the Minds of the Next Generation"

"At other academies, children are only taught
how to survive. Reading skills, mathematics,
art and music lessons — such a waste of a
student's time! Here at the Learning Institute
for the Very Enlightened, we show our students
how to L.I.V.E.!"

— *Mr. Curtain, Founder of L.I.V.E.*

ACCEPTED

RULES OF THE INSTITUTE

1. There are no rules here!

2. You can wear whatever you like. However, trousers, shoes, and shirts are required at all times. Messengers and Executives must wear their uniforms, including tunics and sashes.

3. You don't have to bathe if you don't want to. Simply be clean every day in class. When it comes to personal hygiene, there are unavoidable dangers that must be avoided at all costs.

4. You may stay up as late at night as you wish. Lights are turned off at 10:00 PM, and you must be in your room at that time.

5. You are free to go where you please. Please note, however, that you must keep to the paths and the yellow-tiled corridors. Also, leaving the grounds is not permitted at any time.

6. Eat whatever you want, whenever you want. Our Helpers are available to prepare your favorite delights. Meal hours are posted outside the cafeteria. Latecomers are not permitted.

7. You will be called by the name you prefer. Of course, nicknames are not tolerated unless they are official.

8. Mr. Curtain and his actions are not to be questioned.

Constance Contraire

FOUNDING MEMBER,
THE MYSTERIOUS BENEDICT SOCIETY

Achievements	Has never agreed to do anything
Expertise	Poetic talent, coupled with extreme mental sensitivity
Habits	Grumbling, protesting, demanding sweets, and napping
History	Formerly lived in hiding in a storage room in the Brookville Library
Family	Mr. Benedict, Rhonda Kazembe, and Number Two

This page from one of Constance's notebooks provides insight into that rare pair of qualities that defines her: unruliness and poeticism.

Loud Crowd

Old Mold

Lone Throne

Thin Skin

Hair Flair

Ancient Fungal blah blah

At least I'll have a ha ha ha

Wild Child

Brain Pain

Fake Quake

Bloom Room

Rock Jock

"Rules and schools
are tools for fools —
I don't give two mules
for rules!"

STICKY'S Sweet

A photographic memory lets nothing go unnoticed,
as one of our favorite poems by Constance reminds us.

Why don't you leave? (Being a work in free verse)
BY CONSTANCE CONTRAIRE

O, why don't you leave?
It is winter and the flowers are gone, why do you not join them?
It is cold, all warmth has fled, why do you not follow it?
You speak and speak, the air is filled with your words,
But your words are meaningless —
Why not fill the air with youlessness instead?
I see you are angry about something I said.
I hear you say I have a problem.
But my problem is that I can see you and hear you,
For you have not gone, and will not go.

O, why do you not leave?
Why, when I insist that I wish to be left alone?
You say you will not leave until I give back your candy,
But how do you know the candy was not mine?
How do you know that I did not purchase it with my own money?
How do you know that I did not purchase it with my own money?
Why must you irk me with your questions and demands?
I wish to be alone!
We can discuss your candy later, after you have gone,
Just as your candy has gone. Yes, gone! For I have eaten it.
O, now you go? Now you leave, with a slamming of the door?
O, why did I not tell you before?

BEFORE

AFTER

Which of Sticky's sweets did Constance swipe?

Ducts and
DECOYS

*In light of Kate's particular affection for traveling through
heating ducts, we decided to let this one squeeze through.*

By connecting only two of these ducts, you will be able to
crawl from one room to the other. But which ducts are the
ones that fit properly?

Circle the two ducts you need.

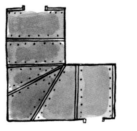

A.

B.

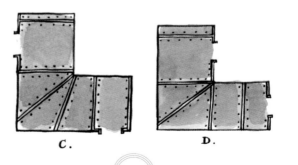

C.

D.

THREE Ways OUT

*When this appeared as part of the very first test,
everyone failed to see the bigger picture — everyone, that is, except
a girl dressed all in yellow. Her name was . . .
well, let's just say it was Number Two.*

This room is completely empty and normal in every way.
You have nothing in your possession except
a small screwdriver.
There are exactly three ways out.
What are they?

1. _ _ _ _ _

2. _ _ _ _ 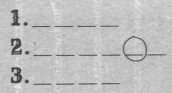 _

3. _ _ _ _ _

A

Is for Apple

*If you think back, you may realize that you can
recognize even the most complex of patterns
in a matter of seconds.*

Number Two almost never sleeps, and because such
wakefulness requires a great deal of energy, she is almost
always eating. As a very orderly person, she has been known
to follow a regimen that places special emphasis on what she
eats, how often, and in what order.

Here is Number Two's record of what she ate
in one twenty-four-hour period.
Unfortunately, she was forced to violate her own dietary
regimen exactly once during this period, due to an
unavailability of ingredients at our local market.

Which food violated Number Two's regimen?

— — — —◯— —

SUNDAY

12:07 AM	zucchini sticks	12:01 PM	muffin
12:53 AM	yogurt	12:47 PM	lamb chop
1:32 AM	almonds	1:36 PM	kumquats
3:09 AM	walnuts	2:54 PM	jam and toast
4:22 AM	vegetable smoothie	3:40 PM	ice cream
		5:23 PM	halibut
6:01 AM	udon noodles	6:19 PM	grapes
6:46 AM	tuna salad	6:58 PM	French onion soup
7:15 AM	salami		
8:07 AM	rye bread with cheese	7:18 PM	egg (hard-boiled)
		8:35 PM	dandelion salad
8:39 AM	quiche	9:15 PM	crackers
9:43 AM	potato (baked)	9:37 PM	banana
9:59 AM	orange	11:56 PM	apple
10:32 AM	nachos		

"There are tests,"
said Mr. Benedict,
"and then there are tests."

TELEGRAM

MISSION (TO) INTERCEPT TEN MEN SUCCESSFUL STOP DISGUISED MYSELF AS JANITOR AT KAKUTO LABORATORY STOP THIRTY THREE PENCILS EVADED STOP ONE MOP DISCHARGED STOP APOLOGIES TO JANITOR FOR THE MESS STOP

URGENT

Milligan

SPECIAL AGENT

Achievements Evaded 873 pencils in the line of duty; saved the lives of the Mysterious Benedict Society members on more than one occasion; has never done another person irreparable bodily harm

Expertise Master of disguise; extraordinary mental and physical fortitude and creativity

History Captured on a mission more than ten years ago and suffered near-total amnesia; went to work for Mr. Benedict after escaping captors; regained memory in final hours on Nomansan Island, including recognizing his daughter

Finding MILLIGAN

Even when we did not know exactly who Milligan was,
we knew what he was made of. This challenge was designed
by Reynie in his honor.

Amid all the finger-pointing
Find the Milligan you can trust
Though he hides among the crowd
His sentries are equally just

Once you have found Milligan, enter his location.

—◯—

continued

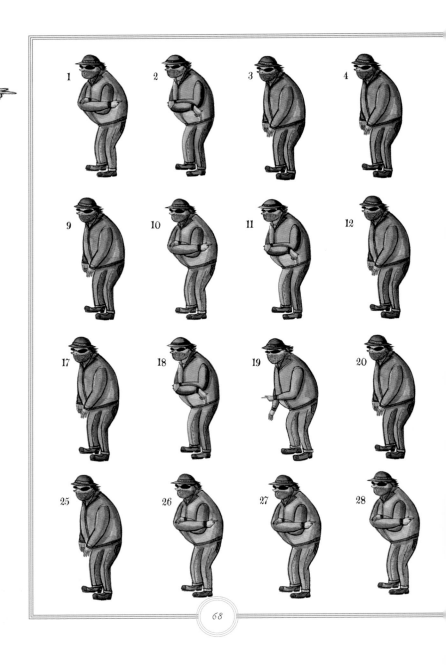

continued

"Will this test be any harder than the last one?"
Kate asked, with a show of bravado.

"Some find it quite difficult," said Rhonda.
"But you should all be able to do it
with your eyes closed."

"Will it be scary?" Sticky asked,
almost in a whisper.

"Maybe, but it isn't really dangerous,"
Rhonda said, which did nothing
for Sticky's confidence.

"Who goes first?" Reynie asked.

"That's an easy one," Rhonda answered. "You."

S.Q.'s
VOCABULIZATION

We must never give up on the S.Q.'s of the world, whose good natures sometimes lead them to do that which they do not mean.

S.Q. is often confused.
In fact, he routinely mangles his words.

For each sentence spoken by S.Q.,
can you figure out what two similar words
he might possibly mean?

1. "I'm simply astoundished!"

a_____d   a_____d

2. "Let's inspectigate!"

i_____t   i_____e

3. "That seems very complexicated."

c_____x   c_____d

4. "How infuritating!"

i_____g   i_____g

5. "This is most unsuitisfactory."

U_____e   U_____y

6. "I'm very disperturbed."

d_____d   p_____d

7. "Mr. Curtain is quite innoventive."

i_____e   i_____e

8. "This is cataclystrophic!"

c_____c   c_____c

9. "I find such behavior repellsive."

r_____t   r_____e

10. "I'm baffuddled."

b_____d   b_____d

TAKE THE SHORTCUT!

THE SPEEDIEST CARGO SHIP IN HISTORY

★

FIVE TIMES AS FAST AS ANY IN ITS CLASS

★

CAN CROSS THE ATLANTIC IN TWO DAYS FLAT!

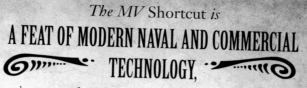

The MV Shortcut *is*

A FEAT OF MODERN NAVAL AND COMMERCIAL TECHNOLOGY,

its every detail designed with speed in mind.

⭐ Hydrodynamic hull design reduces resistance on the water by over 30 percent.

⭐ Jet propulsion system efficiently produces speeds upward of 60 knots.

⭐ Patented "Cargo-to-Go" system means containers can be rolled on and off in a fraction of the time normally required.

The MV Shortcut *is not just the fastest way, it's also the most secure, with a high-security cargo hold designed by world-renowned vault designer Hans Warrilow. Large enough to hold the ship's entire crew, constructed of three-foot-thick expanded metal, and lockable from the inside in case of attack, nothing could keep your precious cargo safer.*

CAPTAIN PHILIP NOLAND AND HIS CREW

INVITE YOUR CARGO TO JOIN THE MV *SHORTCUT*'S MAIDEN TWO-DAY ATLANTIC CROSSING FROM STONETOWN HARBOR TO

THE PORT OF LISBON, PORTUGAL.

DEPARTING AT 4:00 PM

September 19

TOP SECRET

THE TEN MEN

WHO ARE THEY?

The Ten Men are well-dressed professionals who do Mr. Curtain's dirty work. They were previously known as Recruiters, due to their role in "recruiting" — often just another word for kidnapping — orphans and runaways to bring to the Learning Institute for the Very Enlightened.

WHY ARE THEY DANGEROUS?

The Ten Men are believed to have ten ways of hurting their victims — thus, their name. Many of their weapons are thought to have been designed by Mr. Curtain himself. Each Ten Man carries a briefcase containing an arsenal of dangerous supplies: razor-sharp pencils, poisonous chewing gum, a laser pointer that fires a real laser, and so on.

HOW CAN THEY BE IDENTIFIED?

Since they dress like common businessmen, the Ten Men frequently go undetected. However, one identifying feature is the presence of shockwatches — dangerous accessories that emit wires capable of electrifying their victims — on both wrists. Another is their eerily calm behavior. Some Ten Men have been known to speak to their intended victims in childish barnyard terms, such as "Ducky" or "Chickie."

Salamander
vs.
WHISPERER

*Kate has an uncommon knack for calculating distances
and other spatial relationships — but even those
without her gifts can bounce back.*

Near a high reflective wall, you succeed in taking
control of Mr. Curtain's Salamander and discover
that it has been modified with a special transmitter.
This transmitter emits a spherical energy field
capable of disabling any electrical device.

Your mission is to disable the Whisperer,
which is positioned nearby.

Where should you aim the
transmitter on the reflective wall
in order to disable
the Whisperer?

_____

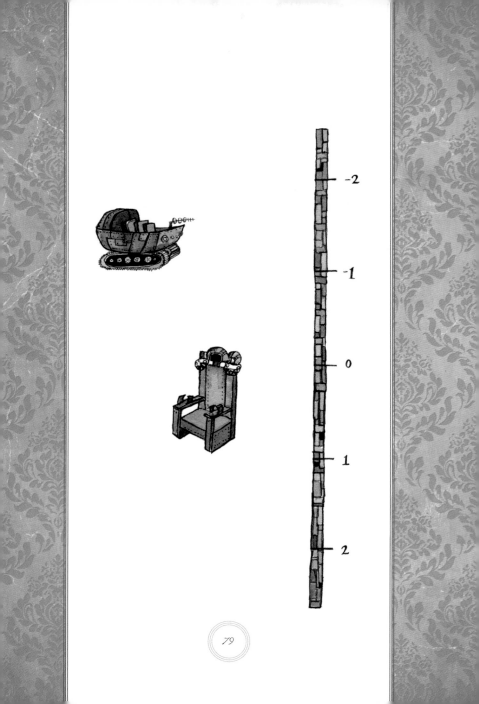

-2

-1

0

1

2

Madge's Bird's-Eye View

Few skills are more valuable than the ability to see things from an entirely different perspective.

Circling high overhead, Kate's falcon, Madge, spies this scene far below.

Where is Kate?

K

F

I

C

J

A

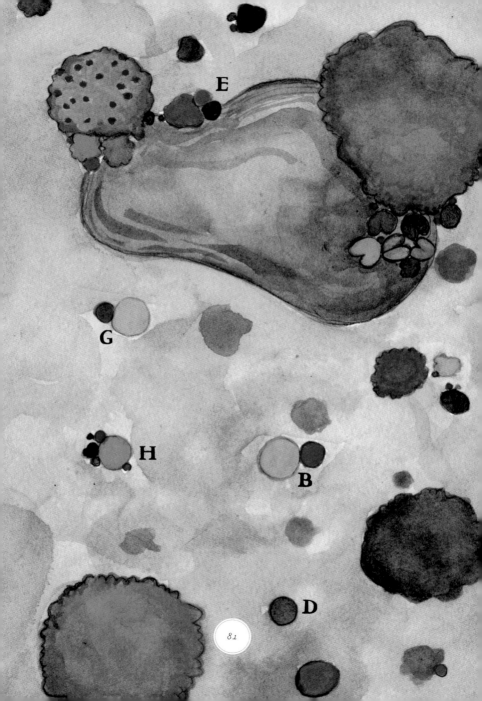

Rare Pair

Only someone of Constance's temperament could reduce an entire impenetrable book into two amusing words that rhyme.

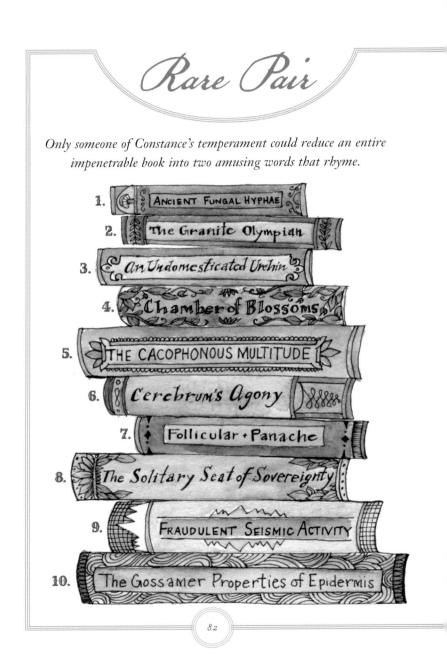

1. ANCIENT FUNGAL HYPHAE
2. The Granite Olympian
3. An Undomesticated Urchin
4. Chamber of Blossoms
5. THE CACOPHONOUS MULTITUDE
6. Cerebrum's Agony
7. Follicular Panache
8. The Solitary Seat of Sovereignty
9. FRAUDULENT SEISMIC ACTIVITY
10. The Gossamer Properties of Epidermis

Sticky once attempted to explain to Constance just a few of the 1,737 books found in Mr. Benedict's study. It pleased him greatly when she appeared to be taking studious notes.

However, when at last Constance revealed what she'd been writing, he saw that she had turned each title into nothing more than two rhyming words.

Like Constance, translate each book's title into a pair of amusing one-syllable words that rhyme.

1. __ __ __   __ __ __ __

2. __ __ __ __   __ __ __ __

3. __ __ __ __   __ __ __ __ __

4. __ __ __ __ __   __ __ __ __

5. __ __ __ __   __ __ __ __ __

6. __ __ __ __ __   __ __ __ __

7. __ __ __ __   __ __ __ __ __

8. __ __ __ __   __ __ __ __ __○

9. __ __ __ __   __ __ __ __

10. __ __ __ __   __ __ __ __

Together, privately, the children
thought of themselves as the
Mysterious Benedict Society,
and as such they had held a
great many meetings — some in
extraordinarily dire circumstances.

Tamil
SQUARES

*Miss Perumal used these simple puzzles from her childhood
to teach Reynie how to think in Tamil, her native tongue.
Now it's your turn.*

A complete Tamil square includes all of
the numbers 1 through 9.
(If you are unfamiliar with Tamil numbers,
please consult the Helpful Resources.)

Solve each Tamil square by filling in the
missing numeral in the middle.
The first has been done for you.

continued

எ	கை	க
உ		ங
கூ	ரு	அ

க	ங	ச
அ		கூ
எ	கூ	ரு

உ	கூ	எ
ரு		அ
கூ	ங	ச

continued

கூ	ச	அ
க		எ
ங	உ	கூ

ரு	கூ	உ
ங		க
ச	எ	அ

Jackson *and* Jillson's
NURSERY RHYME

Executives who are obstructive can be very instructive.

> Jackson and Jillson went up the hillson
>
> To fetchet a pailet of water.
>
> Jackson fell downdown and brokedown his crowndown
>
> And Jillson came trampleson after.

What is the correct spelling of the misspelled word?

◯— — — — — — — — — —

Shortcuts *and* Sudden Turns

*This gem comes from our
old friend Cannonball!*

Cut through the clutter
Then meet in the gutter
The bullfrog will shudder
To lose his bread and butter!

What did you find?

___ ◯ _____

CLUTTERTCLUTTERUCLUTTERRCLUTTE
RNCLUTTERTCLUTTERHCLUTTERECLUT
TERCCLUTTEROCLUTTERRCLUTTERNCL
UTTERECLUTTERRCLUTTERS

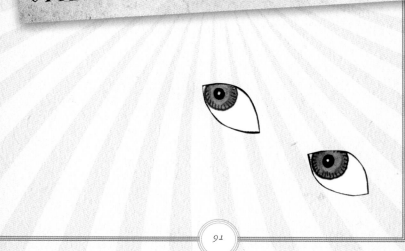

THE
Table of Contents

See the Table of Contents.

In a book like this, the Table of Contents
tells you where to go.

It lists proper names and page numbers.

It appears before the beginning but after the title.

And it's really quite simple to use.

What's found in the Table of Contents?

Unidentical Twins

Our most basic assumptions sometimes mislead us.

A kindhearted genius had a long-lost twin brother
who was an inventor.

What relation was the kindhearted genius to the brother
who was an inventor?

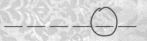

Through THE Looking Glass

*Upon reflection, the solution may
be right in front of you.*

You are a spy at Mr. Curtain's Learning Institute
for the Very Enlightened (L.I.V.E.),
and you have been caught. In fact, a mob of
Executives is now chasing you through the halls
of the student dormitory.

Milligan appears suddenly from a student
washroom and pulls you inside. By the sink, he
thrusts a piece of paper into your hand and says,
"I'll hold them off while you escape," before
disappearing back into the hallway.

Here is the piece of paper.

6n1H3d

70771M

ZI

n39O

7006

Where is the secret door?

_ _ _O_ _ _   the   _ _ _ _ _ _ _

GOVERNMENT DOSSIER

LEDROPTHA CURTAIN

WHO IS HE?

Mr. Curtain is the founder of the Learning Institute for the Very Enlightened (L.I.V.E.), a secluded boarding school now known to be the source of telepathic transmissions during the Emergency. In addition to inventing the Whisperer, a highly advanced machine capable of mind control, Mr. Curtain has been responsible for a series of significant scientific breakthroughs, including tidal turbine energy and mobile noise cancellation. Unfortunately, he appears determined to use his genius for nefarious purposes.

WHAT DOES HE WANT?

In a word, control. Ledroptha Curtain has hatched one bold plan after another in hopes of seizing power over the global population. His grand mind-control scheme, code-named "the Improvement," would have affected billions — as would his quest to acquire the fabled plant known as duskwort, which is allegedly capable of putting anyone to sleep.

HOW CAN HE BE IDENTIFIED?

With some difficulty, because Mr. Curtain is now known to have an identical twin: the brilliant Nicholas Benedict. Notably, however, Mr. Curtain almost always wears mirrored sunglasses and travels in a specially equipped wheelchair in order to hide his narcoleptic condition.

Fortunately, my brother, Ledroptha, never had a chance to use the pamphlets discovered on Nomansan Island. But did you notice what the title he hoped to bestow upon himself really stood for?

OFFICIAL ADVISORY
of the Public Health Administration
ⓈUDDEN AMNESIA DISEASE

Just what *is* Sudden Amnesia Disease (SAD)? SAD is an extremely contagious disease that causes total memory loss in those who contract it.

What's being done about it? Although the origin and cure of this disease have yet to be found, they're being investigated by a group of experts headed by none other than Ledroptha Curtain, the highly regarded scientist and our newly named Minister And Secretary of all The Earth's Regions. SAD cases are admitted for free care at the Amnesia Sanctuary on Nomansan Island, a state-of-the-art facility where patients live comfortably, under strict quarantine, while the cure for their disease is sought.

Am *I* a SAD case? Are my neighbors? A common first symptom of SAD is the belief that one hears children's voices in one's head. The onset of this symptom is most sudden, and once it has begun, it persists without interruption until amnesia sets in.

Already feeling better!
A SAD case jokes around with our friendly doctors.

"As it so happens, however, I now find myself in the presence of the best possible team of children I could ever hope for — indeed, have long hoped for — and with not a minute to lose. In other words, you are our last possible hope. You are our *only* hope."

WELCOME TO
MEMORY TERMINAL

Challenges like this, which require you to "spot the difference,"
were favored by Number Two when she was younger.
They provide an exceedingly simple and effective method
for honing one's observation skills.

The Memory Terminal is filled with hundreds of machines
called Sweepers. As part of Mr. Curtain's plan for the
Improvement, these machines are to be used to bury
the memories of millions around the globe.

However, the key to his entire plan is the Whisperer,
a far more sophisticated, one-of-a-kind, delicately balanced
invention that responds only to Mr. Curtain's strict
mental direction. But in a sea of Sweepers, how can
you tell which is the Whisperer?

Consider the next two pages.

Which one is the Whisperer?

———

continued

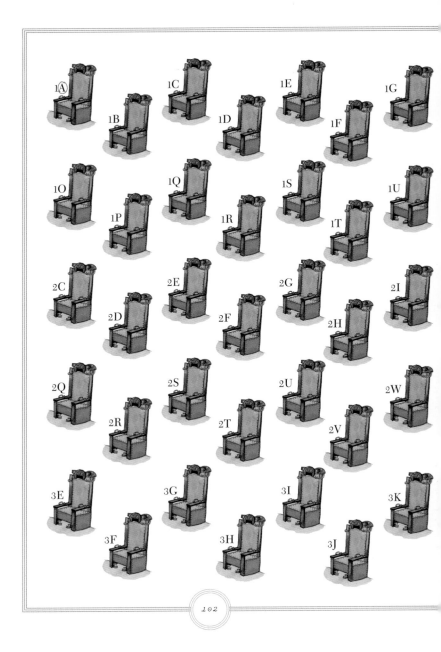

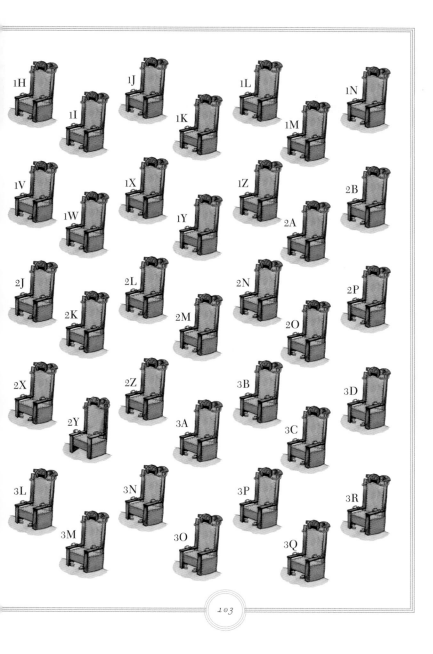

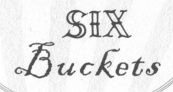

SIX Buckets

Reynie conceived this challenge while pacing in his room, inspired by Kate's red bucket before it was modified with a flip-top. Let us see how your thinking stacks up.

Six buckets are arranged before you,
as seen on the opposite page.

How can you make two lines, each with four buckets,
by moving only one bucket?

Which bucket will you move?

To which position?

—

y z a b c

d e f g h

i j k l m

n o p q r

s t u v w

LIMERICKS *and* ACCUSATIONS

Initially, you might find little worth reading
in Constance's poetry — but then you grow to appreciate
her mischievous sense of humor.

(This exercise was the result of an assignment given
to Constance as part of her lessons.
It is reprinted here without permission.)

1.

There once was a sturgeon named Sticky,
Whose scales were all slimy and icky.
A most nasty fish,
But I got my wish,
And wishers must never be picky!

2.

There once was an ingrate named Kate,
Who disliked what was put on her plate,
Just because I had taken
Every bit of her bacon
And replaced it with peas, which I hate!

3.

Now here is a blockhead named Reynie.
Often he secretly thinks I am whiny.
Tonight I shall sneak (to) his bed,
Mess not with his mind but his head.
Even to Sticky, his scalp will seem shiny!

Which one of these limericks was clearly NOT
written by Constance Contraire?

———

Rhonda Kazembe

ASSOCIATE TO MR. BENEDICT

Achievements   Trained the members of the Mysterious Benedict Society; faithfully supported Mr. Benedict in all of his endeavors

Expertise   Varied, with a memory nearly as good as Sticky's and a very even temperament

History   Born in Zambia; brought to Stonetown as a child

Recollections
and
Lucky Predictions

This was one of the first exercises Rhonda ever created herself, shortly after beginning her studies with us.

Before turning the page, study this number carefully.
Perhaps you will find it easy to memorize.

71421283542495 6637

continued

Without referring to the previous page, complete
the number below.

7142_____

What is the nineteenth number in the sequence?

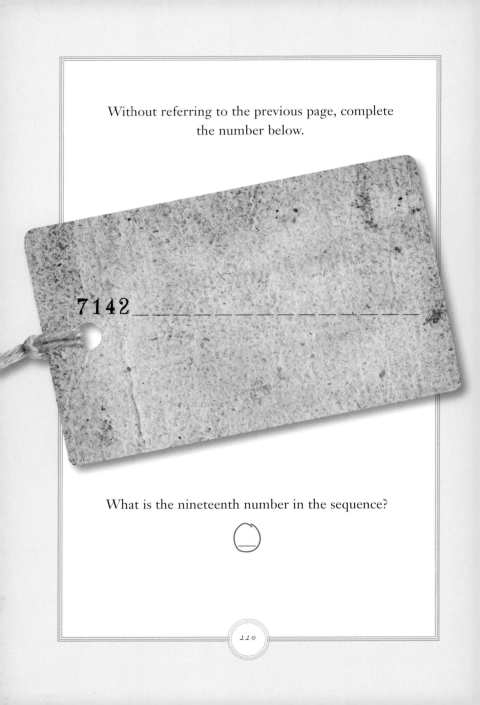

DR TH CUR

THE
SHOW MUST Not
GO ON

Whenever someone gets in a flap,
turn it to your advantage.

Mr. Curtain's Executive Martina Crowe has
decided to lecture you about how much she
dislikes you, as well as other things she hates.
Because she hates so many things,
it promises to be a very long and tedious
lecture, and she has procured a magnificent
theater for the occasion, using proceeds
from Mr. Pressius's diamond scam.

What is the quickest way to
end Martina's lecture?

_ _ _ _   _ _ _

_ _◯_ _ _ _

PROCESSES and ELIMINATIONS

Few people notice everything. Fewer still notice what is missing.

One person compiled the personal profiles found
throughout this book.
Which of the following people was it?
Enter the number below.

1. Mr. Benedict

2. Number Two

3. Rhonda Kazembe

4. Milligan

5. Reynie Muldoon

6. Sticky Washington

7. Kate Wetherall

8. Constance Contraire

And yet, in these last days, he'd become friends
with people who *cared* about him, quite above
and beyond what was *expected* of him.
With perfect clarity he remembered Reynie
saying, "I need you here as a friend." The effect of those
words, and of all his friendships, had grown
stronger and stronger, until — though he
couldn't say *why* he didn't feel mixed up
now — at the most desperate moment yet,
he knew it to be true. There was bravery
in him. It only had to be drawn out.

THIRD ISLAND PRISON

With its perfect symmetry — four identical wings, each four stories high, surrounding a bleak courtyard — Third Island Prison is an easy place to get lost.

One of the Ten Men has hidden an exploding calculator somewhere within the grounds of Third Island Prison. It is set to go off in less than thirty-three minutes.

Will you find it in time?

At your disposal is this coded transmission, which we were fortunate enough to intercept.

NTA   OHS   RET

Combined with this transmission, you have a map, which, beginning from the top and proceeding row by row, provides a comprehensive view of the grounds.

continued

In what area is the exploding
calculator hidden?

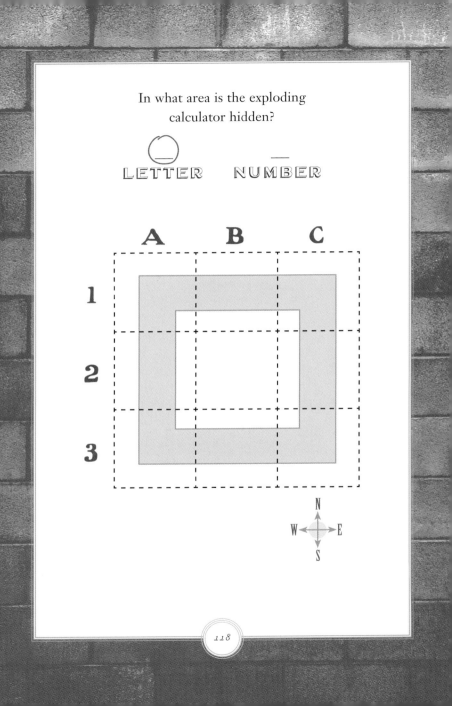

LETTER   NUMBER

THE CAPTAIN'S
Coordinates

*As Captain Noland will tell you, one's destination
is rarely found exactly as expected.*

Turn the world upside down
Though it's north of the equator,
And although English is spoken there,
Let calculation be your translator.

COORDINATES

32° 17' 39"

Where is it?

— — ◯ — — —

GOVERNMENT DOSSIER

TOP SECRET

MR. CURTAIN'S EXECUTIVES

WHO ARE THEY?

The designation "Executive" was first used by Mr. Curtain at the Learning Institute for the Very Enlightened, where students observed a strict organizational hierarchy. It referred to former Messengers — students chosen to undergo sessions in Mr. Curtain's Whisperer — who were then entrusted with ongoing managerial duties. It is believed that, over the years, Mr. Curtain dispatched dozens of Executives around the globe to prepare for the Improvement, his plan for total mind control. After the events on Nomansan Island, however, he retained only a small cadre of Executives.

HOW CAN THEY BE IDENTIFIED?

At L.I.V.E., Executives were identified by their white tunics, blue pants, and blue sashes, but use of such uniforms fell by the wayside after Mr. Curtain fled Nomansan Island. It is believed, however, that some Executives may be easily confused, due to negative effects suffered from repeated sessions in Mr. Curtain's Whisperer. For instance, the dull-minded S.Q. Pedalian is thought to have received the most sessions in the Whisperer; Martina Crowe, the most sharp-minded and aggressive, may have received the fewest.

WINDOWS and MIRRORS

WINDOWS and MIRRORS

*Reynie and I once discussed the notion that where
most people see mirrors, others see windows. The key, of course,
is to know when there is something behind the glass.*

If this is Mr. Benedict . . .

. . . which one is the mirror?

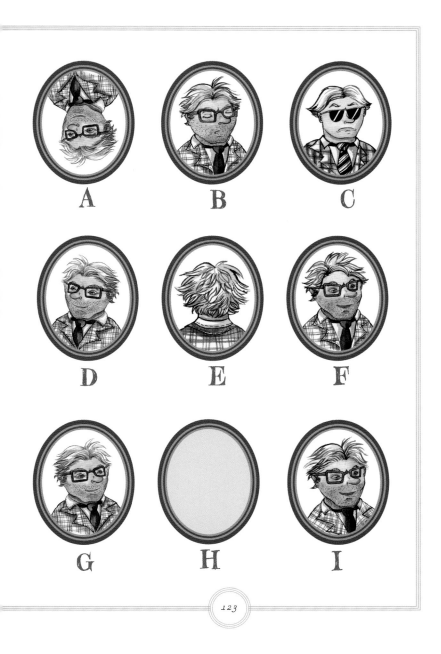

A

B

C

D

E

F

G

H

I

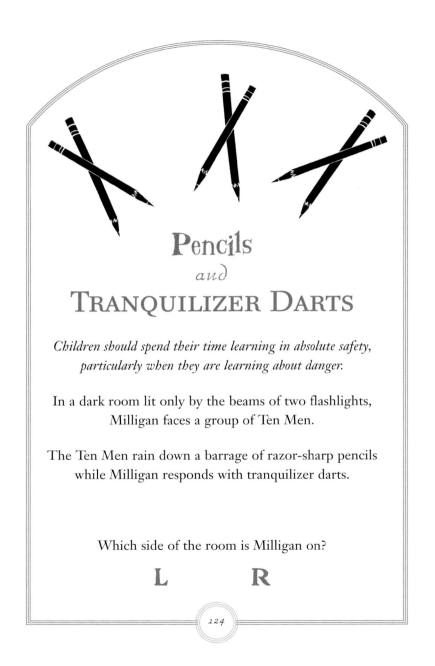

Pencils
and
TRANQUILIZER DARTS

Children should spend their time learning in absolute safety,
particularly when they are learning about danger.

In a dark room lit only by the beams of two flashlights,
Milligan faces a group of Ten Men.

The Ten Men rain down a barrage of razor-sharp pencils
while Milligan responds with tranquilizer darts.

Which side of the room is Milligan on?

L   R

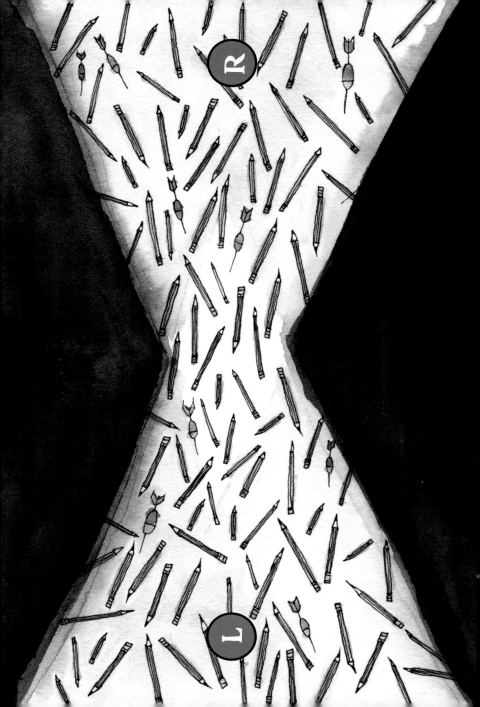

MY BRAIN

Frontal lobe
Impressive! This is the top executive behind my every stroke of genius. Naturally underdeveloped in children.

Amygdala
Highly sensitive to emotions. May be linked to area in cerebral cortex regulating sleep. MUST BE CONTROLLED.

Hippocampus
My gateway to planting thoughts in the minds of others!

Temporal lobe
The invaluable vault where my long-term memories are held. Of course, security in most brains is delightfully lax.

Cerebral cortex
The most intricate and complex area of my brain. I cannot hope to re-create it...only to harness its extraordinary power.

Over my objections, Rhonda insisted that we include this
commendation from my service long ago as a code breaker.
No doubt she thought you would be amused to see a picture
of me in my younger days. At the time, I was no less proud of
orchestrating the inclusion of a small hidden message for a friend.
An agreeable clerk in the Commendations office evidently found
me as persuasive as our wartime enemy did.

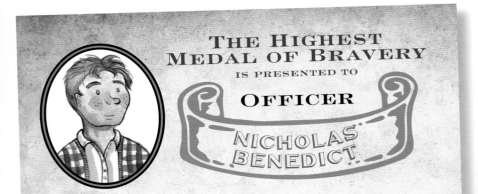

THE HIGHEST
MEDAL OF BRAVERY
IS PRESENTED TO

OFFICER

NICHOLAS BENEDICT

ORDER OF THE CIPHER
U.S. NAVAL INTELLIGENCE

FOR HIS SELFLESS SACRIFICE, IN ENDANGERING HIS
OWN FREEDOM FOR THAT OF LIEUTENANT COMMANDER
PHILIP NOLAND AND THEN UTILIZING UNMATCHED
POWERS OF PERSUASION TO SECURE THEIR SWIFT
RELEASE BY THE ENEMY UNDER HOSTILE CONDITIONS.

SECRETARY OF THE
U.S. NAVY

PRESIDENT OF THE UNITED
STATES OF AMERICA

Nicholas Benedict

MENTOR,
THE MYSTERIOUS BENEDICT SOCIETY

Achievements Last century's Malta Incident; received Stimler Prize for Research in Neuroscience and Philosophy; rarely hit his head when falling asleep; thwarted his brother Mr. Curtain's plans for world domination

Expertise Genius

Habits Narcolepsy (uncontrollable bouts of sleep) triggered by strong emotion

History Born in Holland; after his parents died in a laboratory accident, briefly resided with his aunt in America, then in a series of orphanages; earned multiple university degrees; served as a code breaker in U.S. Naval Intelligence

THE
LAST WORD

No doubt you will recall my brother's secret password,
but he was mistaken about what matters most. Good luck to
you! Quickly, now!

The key is in each other
You know how this must end
In Mr. Curtain's nether worlds
On this you must depend

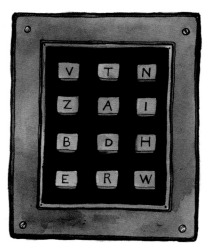

Enter the secret code.

Helpful
Resources

MORSE CODE

A	· —	J	· — — —	S	· · ·
B	— · · ·	K	— · —	T	· —
C	· — ·	L	· · · —	U	· · —
D	— ·	M	— —	V	· · · —
E	— — ·	N	— · ·	W	— · — · —
F	— · · —	O	— — —	X	— · · —
G	· · — ·	P	· — — ·	Y	— · — —
H	—	Q	— — · —	Z	— · ·
I	·	R	· — · ·		

MORSE CODE

A	· —	J	· — — —	S	· · ·
B	— · · ·	K	— · —	T	—
C	— · — ·	L	· — · ·	U	· · —
D	— · ·	M	— —	V	· · · —
E	·	N	— ·	W	· — —
F	· · — ·	O	— — —	X	— · · —
G	— — ·	P	· — — ·	Y	— · — —
H	· · · ·	Q	— — · —	Z	— — · ·
I	· ·	R	· — ·		

1	2	3	4	5	6	7	8	9
க	உ	ங	ச	ரு	கூ	எ	அ	கூ

Reynie smiled to himself. He was
quite familiar with Sticky's habit
of polishing his spectacles when
nervous, and seeing him do so now
was unexpectedly satisfying. There
was a unique pleasure in knowing
a friend so well, Reynie reflected,
rather like sharing a secret code.

STICKY'S GLOSSARY

astoundished. *adj.* a word that does not appear in any of Mr. Benedict's dictionaries, meaning either "astounded" or "astonished"

baffuddled. *adj.* a novel coinage meant to describe feeling "baffled" or "befuddled"

bullfrog. *n.* a slang term meaning "a proud, puffed-up, self-important individual," typically used by Cannonball to refer to wealthy shipowners

cacophonous. *adj.* having a very harsh, discordant, or loud sound

cataclystrophic. *adj.* an unsanctioned portmanteau blending "cataclysmic" and "catastrophic"

cerebrum. *n.* the largest part of the brain, consisting of both the left and the right hemispheres

complexicated. *adj.* a linguistic amalgamation combining "complex" and "complicated"

controle. *n.* a Dutch word meaning "control," which was once used as a secret password by Mr. Curtain

---

disperturbed. *adj.* an accidental mangling of the words "disturbed" and "perturbed"; thought to convey distress

---

epidermis. *n.* the outermost, nonvascular layer of skin; in plants, refers to the outer integument

---

follicular. *adj.* relating to a tiny cavity, usually one that sprouts hair

---

fungal. *adj.* relating to mushrooms, molds, mildews, rusts, or smuts

---

gossamer. *adj.* extremely light, gauzy, fine, filmy, or thin

---

gutter. *n.* a term used in book publishing to indicate the inside margins between two pages that face each other

continued

hyphae. *n.* elements emanating from the spores of fungi

infuritating. *adj.* an awkward neologism meant to describe something that is either "infuriating" or "irritating"

innoventive. *adj.* an unintentional comingling of "inventive" and "innovative"

inspectigate. *adj.* a mistaken construction that jumbles two similar words, "inspect" and "investigate"

multitude. *n.* a very large number of people; a profusion

panache. *n.* a very stylish, flamboyant, enthusiastic, or dynamic manner; élan

repellsive. *adj.* an unwitting verbal entanglement of the adjectives "repellent" and "repulsive"

sovereignty. *n.* royal status or authority; a supreme independent power

transfer protocol. *n.* also known as hypertext transfer protocol, a universal standard for addressing websites on the Internet, including www.mysteriousbenedictsociety.com

undomesticated. *adj.* untamed or wild; unaccustomed to living in accordance with cultural norms

unsuitisfactory. *adj.* an invented word thought to derive from confusion between "unsuitable" and "unsatisfactory"

urchin. *n.* a mischievous young person; distinct from a "sea urchin," which is any echinoderm of the class Echinoidea

vriend. *n.* a Dutch word meaning "friend"

HINTS

PAGE 4
What letters are missing from the classified advertisements?

PAGE 5
Solve the code twice, using each of the Morse codes in the Helpful Resources section. Which side is the right one on?

PAGE 6
Follow the middle of the three digits printed on the page, in the direction of the arrow. Repeat.

PAGE 22
Weather all. Con tray air. Wash in ton. Mull dune.

PAGE 24
See *The Exhaustive Encyclopedia of Sleep*.

PAGE 28
Turn one on its head, and fold another.

continued ▶

PAGE 78
Draw a ninety-degree angle that emanates from the wall. One of its rays must meet the end of the transmitter, while the other ray meets the Whisperer.

PAGE 80
While Moocho holds the pies, Kate has her bucket.

PAGE 82
Look in Constance's notebook.

PAGE 85
Using the chart in the Helpful Resources, write the numbers corresponding to the symbols in each box of a Tamil square. Which number is missing?

PAGE 89
"And Jill came tumbling after."

PAGE 90
Mr. Pressius would not want you to fold each corner into the middle to see what was stolen.

continued

PAGE 92
Look up the page number of this challenge in the book's Table of Contents.

PAGE 93
No one said the kindhearted genius was a man.

PAGE 95
The key lies in the second word, which appears backward. Hold it up to itself to see.

PAGE 101
Mr. Curtain's Whisperer has no leg cuffs.

PAGE 104
Stack *T* in another bucket. But which one?

PAGE 106
Read the first letter of each line.

PAGE 109
Count by sevens.

PAGE 112
Fold the pages together.

PAGE 115
Her name is Pencilla.

PAGE 117
Place the letters into the squares of the map, row by row.

PAGE 119
Read the coordinates upside down on a calculator, like the one hidden on the grounds of Third Island Prison.

PAGE 122
Reverse the picture.

PAGE 124
From which side are the darts originating?

PAGE 130
The end of this word is *end*, even in Dutch, which is spoken in the Netherlands.

"Have you not proven yourselves once again to be the bravest, most resourceful children in the world?"

"Remember, children. For every exit, there is also an entrance."

Upon completion of the preceding exercises,
you are ready to make yours.

$$\overline{}\ \overline{}\ \overline{}\quad \overline{}\ \overline{}\ \overline{}\quad \overline{}\ \overline{}\ \overline{}\ \overline{}\ \overline{}$$

32 32 32   90 113 93   4   4   102 122 73

$$\overline{}\quad \overline{}\ \overline{}\quad \overline{}\ \overline{}\ \overline{}\ \overline{}\ \overline{}\ \overline{}\ \overline{}\ \overline{}$$

115   80 50   18 26 58 58 58 58 30 57 .

$$\overline{}\ \overline{}\ \overline{}\ \overline{}\ \overline{}\ \overline{}\quad \overline{}\ \overline{}\ \overline{}$$

35 110 92 119 60 23   89 95 83

$$\overline{}\ \overline{}\ \overline{}\ \overline{}\ \overline{}\ \overline{}\ \overline{}\ \overline{}$$

104 47 25 62 139 139 29 78

$$\overline{}\ \overline{}\ \overline{}\ \overline{}\ \overline{}\ \overline{}\ \overline{}\ \overline{}\quad \overline{}\ \overline{}$$

76 76 76 107 107 118 67 34   65 65

$$\overline{}\ \overline{}\ \overline{}\quad \overline{}\ \overline{}\ \overline{}\ \overline{}$$

40 40 40   98 5 85 130 .

147

After a few more pages of questions, all of which Reynie felt confident he had answered correctly, he arrived at the test's final question: "Are you brave?" Just reading the words quickened Reynie's heart. Was he brave? Bravery had never been required of him, so how could he tell? Miss Perumal would say he was: She would point out how cheerful he tried to be despite feeling lonely, how patiently he withstood the teasing of other children, and how he was always eager for a challenge. But these things only showed that he was good-natured, polite, and very often bored. Did they really show that he was brave? He didn't think so. Finally he gave up trying to decide and simply wrote, "I hope so."

KEEP READING
FOR A SNEAK PEEK AT

COMING SEPTEMBER 2016

WALKING BACKWARD INTO THE SKY

That summer morning in the Lower Downs began as usual for Reuben Pedley. He rose early to have breakfast with his mom before she left for work, a quiet breakfast because they were both still sleepy. Afterward, also as usual, he cleaned up their tiny kitchen while his mom moved faster and faster in her race against the clock (whose numerals she seemed quite unable to read before she'd had coffee and a shower). Then his mom was hugging him good-bye at the apartment door, where Reuben told her he loved her, which was true—and that she had no reason to worry about him, which was not.

His mom had not even reached the bus stop before Reuben had brushed his teeth, yanked on his sneakers (a fitting term, he thought, being a sneaker himself), and climbed onto the kitchen counter to retrieve his wallet. He kept it among the mousetraps on top of the cupboard. The traps were never sprung; Reuben never baited them, and so far no thieves had reached up there to see what they might find. Not that the wallet contained much, but for Reuben "not much" was still everything he had.

Next he went into his bedroom and removed the putty from the little hole in the wall behind his bed. He took his key from the hole and smooshed the putty back into place. Then, locking the apartment door behind him, he headed out in search of new places to hide.

Reuben lived in the city of New Umbra, a metropolis that was nonetheless as gloomy and rundown as a city could be. Though it had once enjoyed infinitely hopeful prospects (people used to say that it was born under a promising star), New Umbra had long since ceased to be prosperous and was not generally well kept. Some might have said the same of Reuben Pedley, who used to have two fine and loving parents, but only briefly, when he was a baby, and who in elementary school had been considered an excellent student but in middle school had faded into the walls.

Eleven years had passed since the factory accident that left Reuben without a father and his mother a young widow scrambling for work—eleven years, in other words, since his own promising star had begun to fall. And though in reality he was as loved and cared for as any child could hope to be, anyone who followed him through his days might well have believed otherwise. Especially on a day like today.

Reuben exited his shabby high-rise apartment building in the usual manner: He bypassed the elevator and stole down the rarely used stairwell, descending unseen all the way past the lobby to the basement, where he slipped out of a storage-room window. The young building manager kept that window slightly ajar to accommodate the comings and goings of a certain alley cat she hoped to tame, enticing it with bowls of food and water. She wasn't supposed to be doing that, but no one knew about it except Reuben, and he certainly wasn't going to tell anyone. He wasn't supposed to be in the storage room in the first place. Besides, he liked the building manager and secretly wished her luck with the cat, though only in his mind, for she didn't know that he knew about it. She barely even knew he existed.

From his hidden vantage point in the window well, which was slightly below street level and encircled by an iron railing, Reuben confirmed that the alley behind the building was empty. With practiced ease, he climbed out of the window well, monkeyed up the railing, grabbed the lower rungs of the building's rusty fire escape, and swung out over empty space. He hit the ground at a trot. Today he wanted to strike out into new territory, and there was no time to waste. When they'd lived in the northern part of the Lower Downs,

Reuben had known the surrounding blocks as well as his own bedroom, but then they'd had to move south, and despite having lived here a year, his mental map remained incomplete.

Of all the city's depressed and depressing neighborhoods, the Lower Downs was considered the worst. Many of its old buildings were abandoned; others seemed permanently under repair. Its backstreets and alleys were marked by missing shutters, tilted light poles, broken gates and railings, fences with gaps in them. The Lower Downs, in other words, was perfect for any boy who wanted to explore and to hide.

Reuben was just such a boy. In fact, exploring and hiding were almost all he ever did. He shinned up the tilted light poles and dropped behind fences; he slipped behind the busted shutters and through the broken windows; he found his way into cramped spaces and high places, into spots where no one would ever think to look. This was how he spent his solitary days.

It never occurred to him to be afraid. Even here in the Lower Downs, there was very little crime on the streets of New Umbra, at least not the sort you could easily see. Vandals and pickpockets were rare, muggers and car thieves unheard of. Everyone knew that. The Directions took care of all that business. Nobody crossed the Directions, not even the police.

Because the Directions worked for The Smoke.

Reuben headed south, moving from alley to alley, keeping close to the buildings and ducking beneath windows. He paused at every corner, first listening, then peering around it.

He was only a few blocks off the neighborhood's main thoroughfare and could hear some early-morning traffic there, but the alleys and backstreets were dead.

About ten blocks south, Reuben ventured into new territory. He was already well beyond his bounds: His mom had given him permission to walk to the community center and the branch library—both within a few blocks of their apartment—but that was all. And so he kept these wanderings of his a secret.

Despite her excessive caution, his mom was something else, and Reuben knew it. He wouldn't have traded her for half a dozen moms with better jobs and more money, and in fact had told her exactly that just the week before.

"Oh my goodness, Reuben, that is so sweet," she'd said, pretending to wipe tears from her eyes. "I hope you know that I probably wouldn't trade you, either. Not for half a dozen boys or even a whole dozen."

"*Probably?*"

"Almost certainly," she'd said, squeezing his hand as if to reassure him.

That was what his mom was like. Their conversations were usually the best part of his day.

Crossing an empty street, Reuben made his habitual rapid inventory of potential hiding places: a shady corner between a building's front steps and street-facing wall; a pile of broken furniture that someone had hauled to the curb; a window well with no protective railing. But none of these places was within easy reach, when, just as he attained the far curb, a door opened in a building down the block.

Reuben abruptly sat on the curb and watched the door. He held perfectly still as an old man in pajamas stepped outside and checked the sky, sniffing with evident satisfaction and glancing up and down the street before going back in. The old man never saw the small brown-haired boy watching him from the curb.

Reuben rose and moved on, quietly triumphant. He preferred bona fide hiding places when he could find them, but there was nothing quite like hiding in plain sight. Sometimes people saw you and then instantly forgot you, because you were just a random kid, doing nothing. As long as you didn't look lost, anxious, or interesting, you might as well be a trash can or a stunted tree, part of the city landscape. Reuben considered such encounters successes, too. But to go completely unnoticed on an otherwise empty street was almost impossible, and therefore superior. He was reliving the moment in his mind, exulting in the memory of the old man's eyes passing right over him without registering his presence—not once but twice!—when he came upon the narrowest alley he'd ever seen, and made his big mistake.

It was the narrowness that tempted him. The brick walls of the abandoned buildings were so close to each other, Reuben saw at once how he might scale them. By leaning forward and pressing his palms against one, then lifting his feet behind him and pressing them against the other, he could hold himself up, suspended above the alley floor. Then, by moving one hand higher, then the other, then doing the same with his feet, he could work his way upward. It would be like walking backward into the sky.

No sooner had he imagined it than Reuben knew he had to try it. Glancing around to ensure he was unobserved, he moved deeper into the alley. He could see a ledge high above him—probably too high to reach, but it gave him something to shoot for, at any rate.

He started out slowly, then gained momentum as he found his rhythm. Hand over hand, foot over foot, smoothly and steadily. Now he was fifteen feet up, now twenty, and still he climbed. Craning his head around, Reuben saw the ledge not too far above him. Unfortunately, he also saw how difficult it would be to climb onto it—his position was all wrong. He frowned. What had he been thinking? He didn't dare try such a risky maneuver, not at that height. He'd be a fool to chance it.

That was when Reuben felt his arms begin to tremble and realized, with horror, that he had made a terrible mistake.

He hadn't anticipated how drastically his arms would tire, nor how abruptly. It seemed to happen all at once, without warning. Now, looking at the alley floor far below him, Reuben became sickeningly aware of how high he had actually climbed. At least thirty feet, maybe more. The way his arms felt, there was no way he'd make it back to the ground safely. He probably couldn't even get back down to twenty feet.

Thus the action he'd just rejected as being foolishly dangerous suddenly became the only choice left to him, the only hope he had. He had to make the ledge, and by some miracle he had to get himself onto it.

With a whimper of panic, Reuben resumed his climbing. The trembling in his arms grew worse. He could no longer see the grimy, broken pavement of the alley floor below. His vision was blurred by sweat, which had trickled into his eyes and couldn't be wiped away. He was burning up on the inside but weirdly cold on the outside, like a furnace encased in ice; the alley's quirky cross breezes were cooling his sweat-slick skin. Beads of perspiration dripped from his nose and blew away.

In desperate silence he pressed upward. He heard the wind fluttering in his ears, the scrape of his shoe soles against brick, his own labored breath, and that was all. He was so high up, and so quietly intent on climbing, that had any passersby glanced down that narrow alley they'd have noticed nothing unusual. Certainly none would have guessed that an eleven-year-old boy was stretched out high above them, fearing for his life.

As it happened, there were no passersby to see Reuben finally come to the ledge, or to note the terrible moment when he made his fateful lunge, or to watch him struggle for an agonizingly long time to heave himself up, his shoes slipping and scraping, his face purple with strain. No one was around to hear Reuben's gasps and sobs of exhaustion and relief when at last he lay on that narrow ledge—heedless, for the moment, of his bruised arms and raw fingertips. If any passersby had been near enough to hear anything, it would have been only the clatter of startled pigeons rising away above the rooftops. But in the city this was no unusual sound, and without a thought they would have gone on with their lives, reflecting upon their own problems and wondering what to do.

Reuben lay with his face pressed against the cement ledge as if kissing it, which indeed he felt like doing. He felt such immense gratitude for its existence, for its solidity beneath him. After his pulse settled and his breath returned, he rose very cautiously into a sitting position, his back against brick, his legs dangling at the knees. With his shirt he dried his eyes as best he could, wincing a little from the smarting in his scraped fingertips. His every movement was calculated and slow. He was still in a dangerous predicament.

The ledge was keeping Reuben safe for the time being, but it was only a ledge, spattered here and there with pigeon droppings.

When Reuben tried to look up, the wind whipped his hair into his eyes; to keep them clear he had to cup his hands like pretend binoculars. The rooftop seemed miles above him, and might as well have been. Beyond it the early-morning sky was blue as a robin's egg. A perfect summer morning to have gotten stuck on a ledge in a deserted alley.

"Well done, Reuben," he muttered. "Brilliant."

He knew he couldn't get back down the same way he'd come up. He would have to edge around to the back of the building and hope for a fire escape. Otherwise his only option was to follow the ledge around to the street side, try to get in through one of the windows there. If he was lucky, perhaps no one would spot him. But if he couldn't get in, he would have to shout for help. Reuben imagined the fire truck's siren, the fierce disapproval on the firefighters' faces, the gathering crowd—all of it terrible to contemplate, and none of it even half as bad as facing his mom would be.

His mom, who thought he was safe at home in their apartment, reading a book or watching TV or maybe even back in bed. His mom, who even now was on her way to slice and weigh fish at the market, her first and least favorite work shift of the day. His mom, who had never remarried, who had no family, no boyfriend, no time to make friends— meaning Reuben was all she had, Reuben the reason she worked two jobs, Reuben the person for whom she did everything in her life.

His mom, who would not be pleased.

"Oh, let there be a fire escape," Reuben breathed. "Oh, please." Swiveling his eyes to his left, he studied the precious, narrow strip of cement keeping him aloft and alive. It appeared sound enough, no obvious deterioration. A brown crust of bread lay nearby (probably some pigeon's breakfast that he'd rudely interrupted), but that was all—no broken glass or other hazards. His path looked clear.

Reuben began shifting himself sideways, moving left, toward the back of the building. He kept his shoulder blades pressed against the brick wall behind him, his eyes fixed straight ahead at the featureless wall of the building opposite him, just a couple of yards away. He tried very hard not to imagine the dizzying drop below him.

He had progressed a few feet when his hand came down on the crust of bread. Without thinking, he attempted to brush it away. It seemed to be stuck. Glancing down now,

Reuben discovered that the bread crust was actually a scrap of leather, and that it was not in fact resting on the ledge but poking out of the bricks just above it. What in the world? Why would this scrap of leather have been mortared into the wall where no one would ever see it? Was it some kind of secret sign?

Reuben pinched the scrap awkwardly between two knuckles and tugged. It yielded slightly, revealing more leather, and through his fingers he felt an unseen shifting of stubborn dirt or debris, like when he pulled weeds from sidewalk cracks. He tugged again, and a few loose bits of broken brick fell onto the ledge, revealing a small hole in the wall. The brick pieces appeared to have been packed into it.

Reuben took a firmer grip on the leather and gave another tug. More bits of brick came loose. The scrap of leather turned out to be the end of a short strap, which in turn was connected to a dusty leather pouch. Carefully he drew the pouch from the hole and up into his lap.

Not a secret sign. A secret *thing*.

He should wait to open it, he knew. It would be far easier, far wiser to do it after he was safely on the ground.

Reuben stared at the pouch in his lap. "Or you could just be extra careful," he whispered.

With slow, deliberate movements, Reuben brushed away some of the brick dust. The pouch was obviously old, its leather worn and scarred. It was fastened with a rusted buckle that came right off in his hand, along with a rotted bit of strap. He set these aside and opened the pouch. Inside was a small, surprisingly heavy object wrapped in a plastic bread sack. It was bundled up in yet another wrapping, this one of stiff canvas. Whatever it was, its owner had taken great pains to keep it safe and dry.

Reuben unbundled the wrappings to reveal a handsome wooden case, dark brown with streaks of black. Its hinged lid was held closed by a gray metal clasp, the sort that could be secured with a little padlock. There was no lock, though; all Reuben had to do was turn it. He hesitated, wondering what he was about to find. Then he turned the clasp and felt something give. The lid opened with a squeak.

Inside the case were two velvet-lined compartments, both shaped to fit exactly the objects they contained. One of the objects was a small, delicate key with an ornate bow; the other appeared to be a simple metal sphere. Both had the dark coppery color of an old penny and yet, at the same time, the bright sheen of a brand-new one. They were made of a metal Reuben had never seen before. Something like copper or brass, but not exactly either.

Reuben very carefully lifted the sphere from its velvet compartment. It felt as heavy as a billiard ball, though it was not quite as large as one. He turned it in his hands, gazing at it in wonder. What was it? He'd expected that the key would be needed to open it, but there was no keyhole. Looking more closely, he noticed a seam, scarcely wider than a line of thread, circling the middle of the sphere like the equator on a globe, dividing it into two hemispheres.

"So you *can* open it," he murmured.

Holding the sphere in his left hand, Reuben tried, gently, to open it with the other. He used the same gesture that he had seen in countless silly old movies he'd watched with his mom, in which hopeful men drop to a knee and open tiny velvet-covered boxes, proposing marriage with a ring. He imagined he felt every bit as hopeful and excited as those men were supposed to be.

The two hemispheres parted easily, smoothly, without a sound, as if their hidden hinge had been carefully oiled not a minute before. The interior of one hemisphere was hollow, like an empty bowl. It served as the cover for the other hemisphere, which contained the face of a clock. What Reuben had found, evidently, was a pocket watch.

And yet it was a pocket watch of a kind he'd never seen, to say nothing of its quality. Its face was made of a lustrous white material, perhaps ivory, and the hour hand and the Roman numerals around the dial all gleamed black. It was missing a minute hand, but otherwise the parts were all in such perfect condition that the watch might have been constructed that very morning, though Reuben felt sure it was an antique. Indeed, the watch seemed so perfect—so perfect, so unusual, so beautiful—that he almost expected it to show the correct time. But the hour hand was frozen at just before twelve, and when he held the watch to his ear, he heard no telltale ticking.

The key! he thought. Reuben's mom had a music box that his father had given her before Reuben was born. You had to wind it up with a key. It must be the same with this watch.

A closer inspection revealed a tiny, star-shaped hole in the center of the watch face. Could that be a keyhole?

A glance confirmed his suspicion. The key lacked the large rectangular teeth of normal old keys, but rather tapered to a narrow, star-shaped end, small enough to insert into the hole. This was the watch's winding key, no question.

Reuben was tempted. He even laid a finger on the key in its snug compartment. But once again a warning voice was sounding in his head, and this time he listened to it. He might fumble the key, drop it, lose it. Better to wait until he was in a safe place. Better, for once, to resist his impulses. This was far too important.

Reluctantly he closed the watch cover and put the watch back inside the case. He was about to close the lid when he noticed an inscription on its interior: *Property of P. Wm. Light.*

"P. William Light," Reuben muttered, gazing at the name. "So this once belonged to you, whoever you were." He closed the lid, fastened the clasp. "*When*ever you were." For whoever P. William Light was, Reuben felt sure that he'd stopped walking the earth long ago.

Reuben rebundled the case and tucked it back inside the pouch, then stuffed the pouch into the waist of his shorts—no small feat in such an awkward, precarious position. Now he was ready to move.

He took a last look at the hole in the wall, wondering how long the watch had been in there, and who had left it behind. He no longer believed it had anything to do with a bricklayer. No, the watch had been put there by someone like him, someone who found places that were secret to others. It could only have been *found* by someone like him, as well, which made its discovery feel very much like fate.

Just don't blow it by falling, Reuben thought. *Boy finds treasure, plummets to his death. Great story.*

It was with exceeding caution, therefore, that he began to inch sideways along the ledge. A wearisome half hour later he reached the back of the building, only to find that there was no fire escape. No windows, either, and no more ledge.

"Seriously?" Reuben muttered. He felt like banging his head against the brick.

His bottom and the backs of his thighs were aching and tingling. Another hour on this ledge and he'd be in agony. Yet it would take at least that long to reach the front of the building, and possibly longer.

There was, however, a rusty old drainpipe plunging down along the building's corner. Reuben eyed it, then grabbed it with his left hand and tried to shake it. The pipe seemed firmly secured to the wall, and there was enough room between metal and brick for him to get his hands behind it. He peered down along the length of the pipe; it seemed to be intact. He had climbed drainpipes before. Never at anywhere near this height, but if he didn't *think* about the height…

It was as if someone else made the decision for him. Suddenly gathering himself, Reuben reached across his body with his right hand, grabbed the pipe, and swung off the ledge. His stomach wanted to stay behind; he felt it climbing up inside him. Now that he'd acted, the fear was back in full force.

Clenching his jaw, breathing fiercely through his nose, Reuben ignored the lurching inside him and got his feet set. Then, hand under hand, step after step, he began his descent. He went as quickly as he could, knowing he would soon tire. The pipe uttered an initial groan of protest against his weight, then fell silent.

Flakes of rust broke off beneath his fingers and scattered in the wind. Sweat trickled into his eyes again, then into his mouth. He blew it from his nose. Every single part of him seemed to hurt. He didn't dare look down. He concentrated on his hands and his feet and nothing else.

And then the heel of his right foot struck something beneath him, and Reuben looked down to discover that it was the ground. Slowly, almost disbelieving, he set his other foot down. He let go of the pipe. His fingers automatically curled up like claws. He flexed them painfully, wiped his face with his shirt, and looked up at the ledge, so high above him. Had he actually climbed all the way up *there*? He felt dazed, as if in a dream.

Reuben withdrew the pouch from the waistband of his shorts and gazed at it. This was no dream. He began to walk stiffly along the narrow alley, heading for the street. One step, three steps, a dozen—and then he felt the thrill begin to surge through him. He'd made it! He was alive! He'd taken a terrible risk, but he'd come back with treasure. It seemed like the end of an adventure, and yet somehow Reuben knew—he just *knew*—that it was only the beginning.